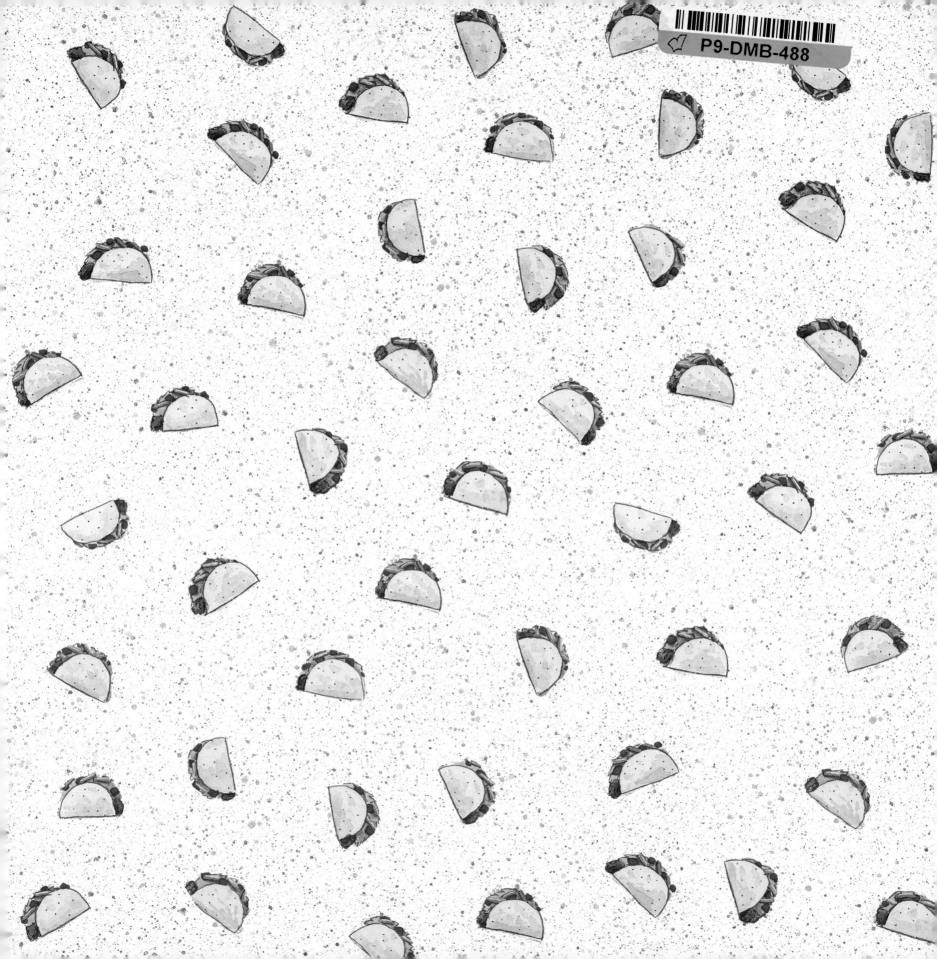

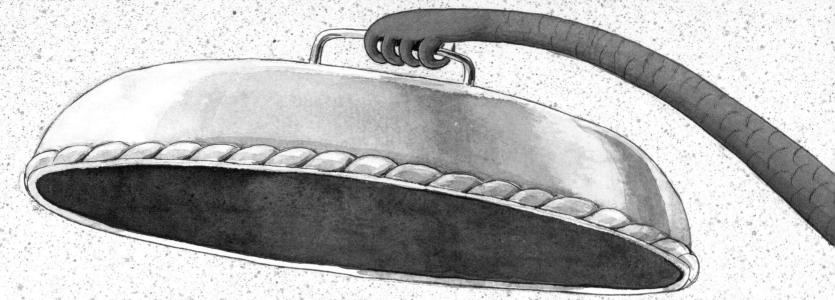

DRAGONS LOVE TACOS

by Adam Rubin

illustrated by Daniel Salmieri

Dial Books for Young Readers an imprint of Penguin Group (USA) Inc.

DIAL BOOKS FOR YOUNG READERS
An imprint of Penguin Young Readers Group • Published by The Penguin Group
Penguin Group (USA) Inc., 375 Hudson Street, New York, NY 10014, U.S.A.
Penguin Group (Canada), 90 Eglinton Avenue East, Suite 700, Toronto, Ontario, Canada M4P 2Y3 (a division of Pearson
Penguin Canada Inc.) • Penguin Books Ltd, 80 Strand, London WC2R 0RL, England • Penguin Ireland, 25 St. Stephen's Green,
Dublin 2, Ireland (a division of Penguin Books Ltd) • Penguin Group (Australia), 250 Camberwell Road, Camberwell,
Victoria 3124, Australia (a division of Pearson Australia Group Pty Ltd) • Penguin Books India Pvt Ltd, 11 Community Centre,
Panchsheel Park, New Delhi - 110 017, India • Penguin Group (NZ), 67 Apollo Drive, Rosedale, North Shore 0632, New
Zealand (a division of Pearson New Zealand Ltd) • Penguin Books (South Africa) (Pty) Ltd, 24 Sturdee Avenue, Rosebank,
Johannesburg 2196, South Africa • Penguin Books Ltd, Registered Offices: 80 Strand, London WC2R 0RL, England

Designed by Jennifer Kelly
Text set in Zemke Hand ITC Std
Manufactured in China on acid-free paper

10

Library of Congress Cataloging-in-Publication Data
Rubin, Adam, date.
Dragons love tacos / by Adam Rubin ; illustrated by Daniel Salmieri.   p. cm.
Summary: Explores the love dragons have for tacos, and the dangers of feeding them them anything with spicy salsa.
ISBN 978-0-8037-3680-1 (hardcover)
[1. Dragons—Fiction. 2. Tacos—Fiction. 3. Food habits—Fiction. 4. Humorous stories.]
I. Salmieri, Daniel, date, ill. II. Title.
PZ7.R83116Dr 2012   [E]—dc23   2011035699

The artwork was created with watercolor, gouache, and color pencil.

To my loving sister Bruce:
smart, beautiful, and full of laughter.
—AR

For Aaron, a wonderful friend.
Thank you for everything.
—DS

Hey, kid!

Did you know that dragons love tacos?

They love beef tacos and chicken tacos.

They love really big gigantic tacos and tiny

little baby tacos as well.

Why do dragons love tacos?

Maybe it's the smell from the sizzling pan.

Maybe it's the crunch of the crispy tortillas.

Maybe it's a secret.

Either way, if you want to make friends with dragons, tacos are key.

Hey dragon, why do you guys love tacos so much?

But wait!

As much as dragons love tacos, they hate spicy salsa even more.

They hate spicy green salsa and spicy red salsa.

They hate spicy chunky salsa and spicy smooth salsa.

If the salsa is spicy at all, dragons can't stand it.

ORLA'S SPICY SALSA

Why do dragons hate spicy salsa?
Well, just one drop of hot sauce
makes a dragon's ears smoke.

Just one single speck of hot pepper makes a dragon snort sparks.
Spicy salsa gives dragons the tummy troubles,
and when dragons get the tummy troubles—
oh boy . . .

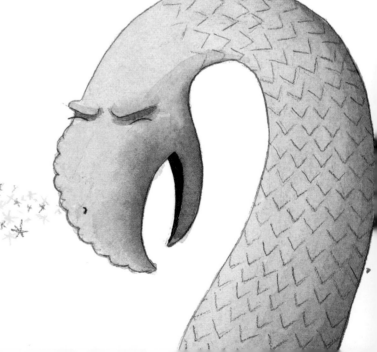

If you want to make tacos for dragons, keep the toppings mild.

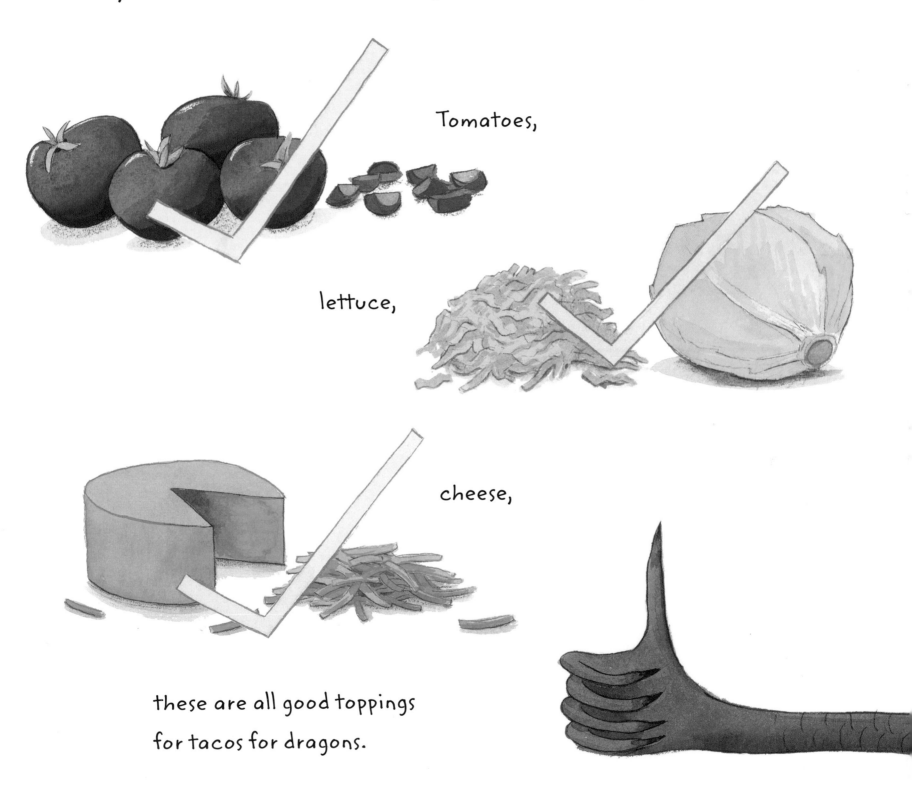

Tomatoes,

lettuce,

cheese,

these are all good toppings
for tacos for dragons.

Hey dragon, how do you feel about spicy taco toppings?

Dragons love parties. They like costume parties

and pool parties.

They like big gigantic parties with accordions

and tiny little parties with charades.

Why do dragons love parties? Maybe it's the conversation. Maybe it's the dancing. Maybe it's the comforting sound of a good friend's laughter.

The only thing dragons love more than parties or tacos, is taco parties (taco parties are parties with lots of tacos).

If you want to have some dragons over for a taco party, you'll need buckets of tacos. Pantloads of tacos. The best way to judge is to get a boat and fill the boat with tacos. That's about how many tacos dragons need for a taco party. After all, dragons love tacos.

Hey dragon, are you excited for the big taco party?

Just remember: Dragons hate spicy salsa.
Before you host your taco party with dragons,
get rid of all the spicy salsa. In fact, bury the spicy
salsa in the backyard so the dragons can't find it.

These dragons love your taco party! They love the music.
They love the decorations. They especially love the tacos.

Congratulations!

It's a good thing you got rid of all that spicy . . .

Wait a second—

what are those little green things in the salsa?

You didn't read the fine print?!

Dragons, listen to me: Do not eat those tacos.

Those little green specs in the salsa? Those are jalapeño peppers—
they are super-spicy! I know you love tacos, dragons, but you are
not gonna love those tacos.

DO NOT LET THOSE DRAGONS EAT THOSE TACOS!!!

Crunch,   crunch,   crunch...

Too late . . .

Why would dragons help you rebuild your house?

Maybe they're good Samaritans.

Maybe they feel bad for wrecking it.

Maybe they're just in it for the taco breaks.

After all, dragons love tacos.

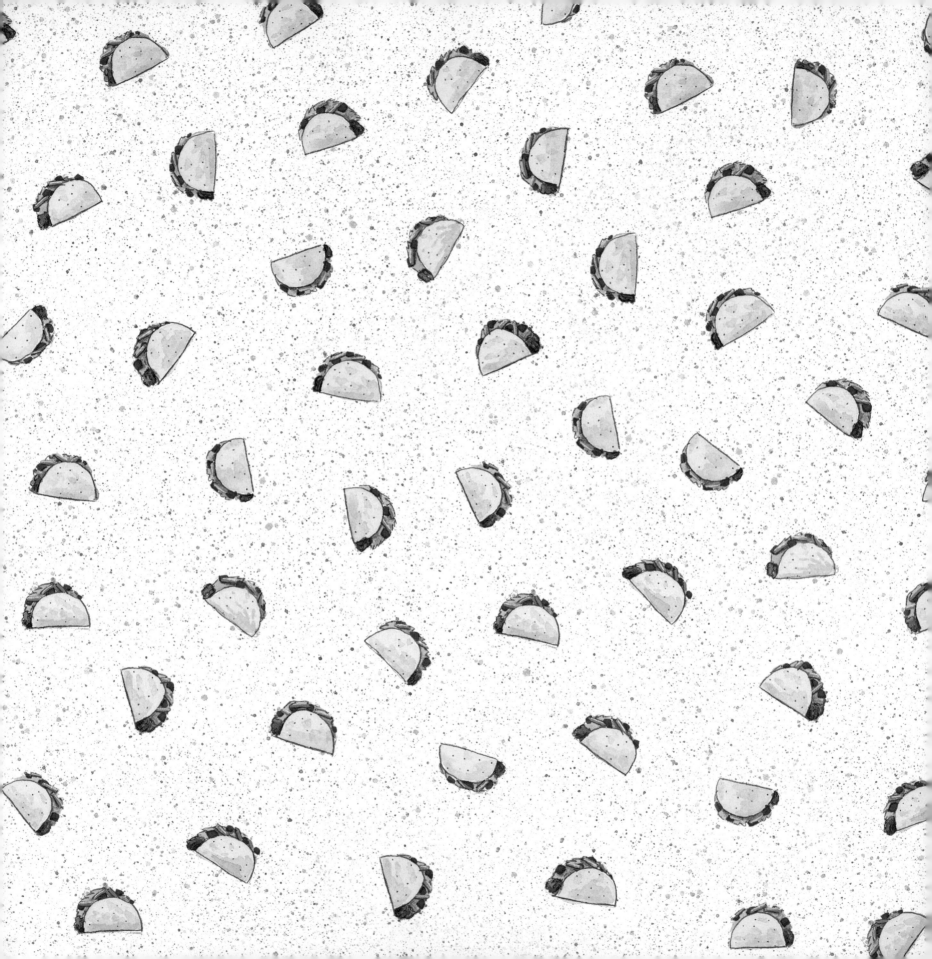